# ELIZA JANE FINDS HER HERO

# ELIZA JANE

## FINDS HER HERO

Eliza Kelley *and* Debra Whiting Alexander

*Illustrated by Patricia Culwell and Jazlin Sobel*

LUMINARE PRESS

WWW.LUMINAREPRESS.COM

Luminare Press
442 Charnelton St.
Eugene, OR 97401
www.luminarepress.com

LCCN: 2023913526
ISBN: 979-8-88679-325-3

For my best friend, Paige.

—EK

For every child who stands out
in an orchard of trees, uniquely gifted and able.
And to the quiet, "deep thinkers" everywhere.

—DWA

# CONTENTS

## A GIRL'S GOTTA TWIRL

*L*IKE a fireball out of nowhere, Eliza Jane Cooper transformed into someone she had only imagined she could be. All in a single day.

Eliza Jane may have been fearless on a horse, but put her in the spotlight and she skittered into hiding as fast as a jackrabbit. She had good reasons for wanting to slip through her days unnoticed. So it came as quite a shock when *presto!* Eliza Jane's life turned into a hair-raising, true-life superhero action movie—starring her—an all-but-invisible ten-year-old girl with tics.

It happened in front of everyone under the bright light of day.

That spring morning, the shiny brass alarm clock beside her bed was oddly quiet. The absence of chiming bells worried her enough to pull her from a spine-tingling dream. She opened one blurry eye, startled to see it was already eight in the morning.

*Eight?! I should have been up an hour ago! I'll be late for school—again.*

Eliza Jane sprang up, eyes blinking rapidly, untangled herself from her twisted sheet, and then sank back with a blissful smile. *Thank goodness it's Saturday.*

If only she could drift back into dreamland. She had been galloping across a grassy field on her horse, Popcorn, in a daring escape. She remembered flying too—soaring into a cloudless Oregon sky, plunging down through pine trees, hovering just above a wild, rumbling river. *Let me keep flying!* A cool mist from the churning white water covered her face, the earthy smell of moss and river rock snaked up her nose. *It was all so real! So satisfying.*

Her favorite part of the dream came next. With a bit of twirling, and whirling, and spinning like a pinwheel, *whoosh!*—Tinklelocks appeared. And it wasn't the first time. Eliza Jane had been magically twirling and whirling and spinning into the superhero of her dreams since she was six. She named her Tinklelocks for the soft whistle tic that sometimes slipped through her own lips, floating on air like tinkling chimes. At the start of fourth grade, Eliza Jane decided it was time to try a more mature, sophisticated name like Savannah Snow, Crystal Star, or Secret Agent Double-O-8. But nothing felt right. Her superhero's name had to remain Tinklelocks, and that was that.

Because all Eliza Jane ever wanted was to be brave. And not to wrestle snortin' bull alligators by the tail. Eliza Jane wanted to be brave to hear the things she pretended not to. Things like, "It's so strange the way she whistles, isn't it?" and "Look at the way she hops. It's not normal," and "That girl needs to quit rolling her eyes. It's weird."

Some days she felt like a three-horned unicorn.

Eliza Jane felt a stirring next to her—dreamland would have to wait until night returned.

Archie Wa-wa, her little black Chihuahua, the most enchanting dog ever, pushed his tender paws against her neck in a long stretch, his tail thumping hard against the pillow.

"Good morning, poo-face." He gave her a wide, toothy doggy grin.

That's right. Archie spoke.

A year earlier, when Eliza Jane first discovered Archie was a talking dog, he had told her: "I say whatever you need to hear. But don't tell anyone. No one would believe it." She wasn't sure she did either. But he kept right on chatting and told her: "Move it! Get out that front door and don't be late for school." The first time Eliza Jane heard those words roll off Archie's long waggling tongue, she had to lean against a wall just to stay upright. Then she did exactly what he said, because who wouldn't? It isn't every day your dog gives *you* commands.

"Poo-face," Archie repeated, his tiny paws still pushing against her neck. "Open your big brown eyes and get boots on the ground! Time for school. You're dawdling again."

"But Archie, it's—"

"Hurry up!" he snapped. "What do I have to do— *bite* you?"

"But we don't..." Eliza Jane let out a long, drawn-out yawn, halting her sentence.

"Look," Archie continued, "I know school makes you jittery—but that's what you have me for, remember?"

Of course she remembered. She had Tourette syndrome. Without trying, her body made sounds and movements adults called "tics" that she had no control over. The doctor explained it was a medical condition that didn't have a cure yet. That's when Eliza Jane's parents found Archie for her. As a trained emotional support dog, he accompanied her wherever she went, including to school. Sometimes, Eliza Jane worried about whistling in the middle of a spelling test, making funny faces and sounds during class, or rolling her eyes at the teacher. But Archie understood she was *not* a troublemaker—it was only her tics. And he helped calm them down. Eliza Jane couldn't be sure, but sometimes she thought he prevented them too.

Medicine and counselors helped Eliza Jane learn to live with all the feelings that came with having tics, but Archie helped her the most. Every time she shared her feelings with him, he listened with kindness, his eyes full of understanding and devotion. She'd always wanted a dog she could talk to.

Eliza Jane yawned again, stretching her arms. "Archie, what I've been trying to tell you is that today is Saturday!"

Archie's ears wiggled with delight. He sighed with pleasure and in less than a minute he rolled belly-up, snoring again.

By eight-thirty, the colorful cowgirls riding broncos on Eliza Jane's curtains danced in the cool breeze from her window. Her big toe caught the sheet when she stumbled out of bed, grabbing for her blue jeans and cowgirl boots. "Giddyup, Archie," she said, sleepily. "No school today. Get ready to ride."

It started out like any other Saturday. Until Eliza Jane met Jacob.

## HOLY POPCORN

*T*HAT morning the sun glimmered everywhere over the small town of Spring Creek. The flower beds sparkled with purple tulips, the sky was as blue as bachelor buttons, and the birds exploded up into the sunshine.

Gigantic trees fanned their woodsy scent on the path down to the horse stalls. Eliza Jane breathed in, enjoying the aroma all the way there. Archie's black coat glistened under a golden beam of light shining down through the leaves above them. Eliza Jane already believed Archie was a heavenly wonder, but by the time that Saturday was over, she would believe it more.

The only other living being who helped Eliza Jane the way Archie did was her horse, Popcorn. She couldn't say how or why, but from the moment she first climbed on top of his creamy tan back and stroked his buttery-white mane, her fears and tics simply melted away. It's true what her mama said—sometimes animals help in ways people can't.

Eliza Jane heaved the rusty metal doors apart on her family's red barn. A flurry of birds scattered across the roof as soon as the doors clanged open. The noise inside was deafening—two donkeys hee-hawing, a giant black stallion neighing in a high-pitched scream, and three mares nickering. Popcorn came eagerly to his stall gate to greet them. When he rubbed his head on hers, Eliza Jane felt the strong bond of love between them. It tingled down her spine.

"Only the bridle today, boy," Eliza Jane told Popcorn. "We're going bareback." He was the only horse she trusted enough to ride without a saddle. Archie rode proudly in a cozy pouch on Eliza Jane's back. He kept watch over the land behind them like a real cowboy.

"I've always liked the view from back here," Archie said. "Not to mention the fresh air. Some goggles might be nice though." Eliza Jane made a mental note: *Find swimming goggles to fit Archie.*

Eliza Jane gave her hair a smart turn and brought it into a twist at the back of her head. She often said her shoulder-length, straight brown hair was the color of a dead mouse. Which is why she dreamed of having the long, flowing, golden curls she imagined Tinklelocks had. *Oh well.* She tucked a few unruly stray hairs under her helmet and hoisted herself on Popcorn's back. She asked him to walk, clucking him forward. "*Good boy.*"

Under cool leafy shadows, they crisscrossed through the orchard between endless rows of hazelnut trees. "Over, over," she signaled to Popcorn. And when they neared a fallen tree, "Steady...steady... *jump!*"

Popcorn sailed over the log with ease, his muscles rippling beneath her legs.

"Holy Popcorn!" Archie howled. "I do love it when we fly."

Eliza Jane stopped in the middle of the orchard to listen to the chitter of squirrels echoing between the

8

trees. Popcorn had taught her many things, but especially how to listen. A few nuts thunked down from the branches, sounding like a giant's boots. It churned up enough fright for Archie that he let out a single *woof*, but the sounds in the orchard didn't scare Eliza Jane. "When my tics happen here they sound like a part of nature," she told Archie.

"As beautiful as the songbirds," he said.

Archie always made Eliza Jane feel more special than she believed she was.

When they meandered out of the orchard, Archie lifted his nose in the air toward squeals of joy. Happy noises rang out from a playground already bursting with children, all of them flittering about like honeybees.

"Whoaaa." Eliza Jane pulled back on Popcorn's reins.

"Wait a minute." Archie's head swiveled right to left. "Why are we going to our school on a *no*-school day?"

"For fun," she told him. "We're only going to the playground—I promise." She believed it when she said it.

Next to the schoolyard gate, morning glories pushed their purple trumpets through the chain-link fence in a cheerful way. Eliza Jane tied Popcorn to a tree and kissed his nose. "Good boy," she said, breathing in his scent, crisp as fresh clover. She reached in the side pocket of Archie's pouch and fed Popcorn a carrot.

"Who are you staring at, Eliza Jane?" Archie asked.

"The boy playing cornhole by himself," she said. "I've never seen him before."

He was a long-limbed boy wearing a blue baseball cap.

Archie pointed his nose in the air again and sniffed. "He looks lonely if you ask me. You should say hello and make friends with him."

"I'm sure he's fine being alone, Archie. Just like I am."

Archie shot her the stink eye. "Maybe that's because you always have me and Popcorn with you."

There was truth to what Archie said, but talking to new people wasn't easy for Eliza Jane. Her tics always got worse. That was the truth, too.

They wandered to a quiet corner of the schoolyard where a massive log sat between two trees. Eliza Jane gave it a closer look. *I wonder if I could walk the length of this trunk without falling.* She hopped up, balancing easily, edging sideways, one foot following the other.

"You're gonna break your whole arm doing that," a familiar voice said calmly.

Eliza Jane lurched, losing all steadiness. She had barely caught her balance again when she saw Ruby standing there, arms folded, her dark curls lifting in the breeze.

*Oh no. Not Ruby.*

"Or you're going to break your whole leg," Ruby added, grinning. "It happened to someone last year. You need to get down from there." Her black eyes looked fierce.

*Mind your own beeswax, Ruby!* That's what Eliza Jane had wanted to say. But couldn't. Being bossed around by a girl like Ruby made her nervous to speak at all.

"You're so quiet," Ruby continued. "I've never seen anyone so shy. It must be why you have a dog with you all the time. By the way, he looks like a little rat."

Eliza Jane's face didn't move. But when she couldn't hold back a tic, she turned her head away, hiding her face while her eyelids fluttered. She reached down her front jeans pocket and grasped a small bottle of essential oils. Sometimes inhaling the fragrances helped her tics go away. She breathed in deep. The soothing blend of cedarwood, lavender, and lemon calmed her tic almost instantly. She turned and watched Archie sniff curiously around Ruby's shoes, snorting like a pig. *Not* a rat.

Ruby's words "shy" and "rat" stuck in Eliza Jane's head. If she had found her tongue, she would've said: "He's not a rat. He's a rare, highly intelligent, trained super dog." She would've flashed a proud smile at Archie and continued. "He was living on the streets when I rescued him off the railroad tracks in a very dangerous city seven hundred miles away! He can't be without me now." At least part of it was true. *If only Archie would speak now. That would show her.*

But Archie wouldn't speak to anyone but Eliza Jane.

11

"No one else gets to have a dog with them during school," Ruby complained. "It's not fair!" And then she bolted away.

"She's wrong," Archie said. "It's always fair when people get what they need. And lucky for me you need me."

"She called me 'shy' too! It's a bad three-letter word, Archie. I hate being called that. You know I'm a deep thinker. *Not* shy."

"You're as deep as they come," Archie said. "Your heart is full of feelings, just the way I like it. And, the *nerve* of her, calling me a 'rat'!"

Archie gave Eliza Jane a sloppy kiss on the nose when the yelling started. A spat had broken out around the fire pole. *It's Ruby again.* Eliza Jane recognized that booming voice anywhere.

Archie stood rooted like the old maple shading them. His ears pointed to the sky.

"How much do you want to bet she's needling the new boy now?" Eliza Jane sighed. She dragged her feet as she walked to the fire pole, complaining under her breath about the way Ruby always had to make a fuss about something. Archie sprang ahead, romping around the pole, yipping and yodeling like she had never heard him yip and yodel before. The whole playground came to a standstill.

Eliza Jane was right. The long-limbed boy wearing a blue baseball cap clung to the top. Shimmying up after him was Ruby, quarreling with him about something.

"It's rude to yell and roll your eyes at me, Jacob!" Ruby roared.

*So that's his name.*

"That's not what I was doing," he said.

When Jacob lost his grip, he slipped down, crashing into Ruby. They dropped with a thud and landed in a heap. Ruby sprang to her feet, her wild black hair bouncing as she stomped around the pole. When Jacob stood, Ruby's hand shot out, two fingers poking him in the chest. "Just because you're new to this school doesn't mean you have to annoy people to get attention." She wheeled around, speaking to everyone watching. "He does this in our class too."

Jacob's forehead crinkled. "I don't want attention. That's the last thing I want." His cheeks turned the color of a red-hot chili pepper.

"And stop making silly faces at me!" Ruby barked. "That's *not* funny."

Jacob groaned. "I didn't mean to, I—"

"You did too!" Ruby snapped. "You're lying!"

Quick as a flash, Archie gave Eliza Jane a sharp kick in the shin with his hind leg. She scooped him up. "I think the kid has tics," he mumbled in her ear. "Shouldn't you say something?"

*If only I could.*

Eliza Jane hadn't meant to keep her condition a secret at school, but it became one anyway. When her teacher had offered to explain what Tourette syndrome was to her class, it made her stomach spin. Especially when she found out a whole lesson had already been planned about it! Naturally, it would be explained that Tourette's wasn't contagious and that tics were caused by the brain. But then what? Eliza Jane imagined her teacher saying, "*Tics are not insects, class! Now, please be good listeners while Eliza Jane tells us all about hers.*" She'd have to talk about eye blinking, eye rolling, skip-hopping, throat sounds, and whistling? *No thanks.*

*And what about all the tics no one sees? Would I have to describe those too?* Some of Eliza Jane's hardest days were when she looked totally fine. At times her skin tickled everywhere. And even her blood felt itchy! When her legs were full of tickles, it was hard not to run, even when it wasn't safe to. She hated it when she did things that weren't safe. How many times had Eliza Jane cried, "I want out of my body!"? *Too many times to count.* The last thing she wanted to do was point out how attention problems, anxiety, fears, anger, and other challenges also went along with Tourette's. Eliza Jane was about as excited to say all that to her classmates as she was to ride a whopping, wild-flying bucking bull. *Not happening.*

With Archie snug in her arms, Eliza Jane had answered her teacher politely. "No thanks. I don't want the class to know about my condition." But what she really meant was: *Are you kidding me? That would make everything worse! I* want *to be invisible.*

At least, she thought she did.

"Eliza Jane?" Archie interrupted her thoughts. "Are you hearing me right now?"

She burrowed her nose behind his ears, his scent as pleasing as fresh corn chips. Ruby and Jacob's angry voices shot through the air again.

"We have a problem here." Archie looked at Eliza Jane square in the face, his eyes like lasers. "It's up to you now."

3

## A BAD CASE OF STAGE FRIGHT

"*W*HAT do you mean it's up to me?!" Eliza Jane dropped her head.

"Jacob has tics and no one understands except you. Shouldn't you say *something*?"

"Well, sure," Eliza Jane whispered, running her thumb around Archie's collar. "Someone should definitely say something. Just not me. I can't speak up."

"Piffle!" Archie snapped.

"It's true," Eliza Jane said in her most convincing voice. "I don't know how."

"Girl—taking action builds confidence and courage. That's true for everyone."

Eliza Jane supposed Archie could be right. It might be true for everyone—except her.

Jacob smacked his ball cap against his thigh. "I hate this school already!" His whole face blazed red now around eyes as blue as a tropical sea. "And I don't lie!" he added. "Well, not usually." He twisted his cap between two tight fists.

Pollen dusted the pine-sweetened air as Jacob sneezed several times, his fingers rubbing the corners of his eyes.

Eliza Jane watched his neck twist, first to one side, then the other. After that, his eyes rolled to the back of his head several times, and he scrunched up his face real tight. It looked painful.

"See? He's doing it again," Ruby said, wagging her finger in disapproval. "Stop doing that!"

But Jacob wasn't to blame. And neither were his allergies. Anyone could see his tics were beyond his control. Anyone who understood tics, that is.

"Honest, I don't mean to be rude," Jacob said.

When he shrugged his shoulders and didn't stop, Eliza Jane knew that was a tic, too.

"No one gets it," he sighed. "I give up."

Jacob looked so sad and tired, Eliza Jane's heart broke.

"He's a big faker," Ruby squawked. "Don't pay any attention to him. You can't believe a thing he says."

But Eliza Jane believed him. She understood more than Jacob knew. She knew he didn't do what he did to be rude. The eye rolling, neck twisting, grimaces, and shrugging—they were tics. And Archie was right. She should've said something. But she didn't know how to say things the way Ruby could. Eliza Jane had tried, but all her words clogged in her throat and wouldn't come out. Like a bad case of stage fright. It can happen to introverts—people who usually like to think more than they like to talk.

"News flash," Ruby said, eyeing Jacob up and down. "No one wants to play with you." And then she called him a hurtful name.

Eliza Jane slapped a hand over her mouth, mortified for him. *That's not true!* She had been called that unkind word and others like it plenty of times herself. *What should I do?* Her heart beat like a drum when she pressed a knuckle to her sweaty temple and tried to think. But her brain felt frozen. She only knew she wanted Ruby to stop, to quit being so unkind, but Eliza Jane didn't have the guts to tell Ruby she didn't know what she was talking about.

"Ruby's right about one thing." Archie locked eyes with Eliza Jane. "No one wants to play with Jacob now. If anyone should be his friend, it's you."

"Archie, just because we both have tics doesn't mean I have to be his friend!"

"I know that," he said. "But if you were Jacob, what would *you* want?" Archie held her gaze until she answered.

"I'd want a friend to help." Eliza Jane bit her lower lip when guilt pressed on her chest. *I'm a stinkin' coward.*

18

Still, Ruby didn't know diddly-squat. She was the one being mean.

*Oh, how I'd like to stick my tongue out at her!*

*Whack.* Eliza Jane banged the trunk of a tree with her heel instead.

*Thank goodness Ruby isn't in my class. If she knew about my tics too, she'd be wagging that finger of hers at me, and no one would want to play with me either!* It was a dreadful thought.

Eliza Jane felt her tics itching to come out. They were getting too strong to hide. She skip-hopped with Archie over to the old maple tree, hid behind its bulky trunk, and let them out where no one could see. Especially Ruby. She patted her body, blinked as much as she needed to, and cleared her throat. She needed to grunt and whistle a few times too.

"I need Tinklelocks," Eliza Jane said, sighing.

"Who?" Archie asked.

"You know, the secret superhero inside me, silly!" Eliza Jane thought he would've known. "All I have to do is twirl and whirl and spin a few times and I turn into her. In my dreams anyway."

Eliza Jane started twirling and whirling, spinning like a pinwheel, just in case. But nothing happened. For some unknown reason, she twirled yet again. "Rattlesticks," she muttered. *What a silly idea. Of course it only happens in my dreams.*

19

Eliza Jane slipped Archie's pouch around her neck and tucked him in against her chest. "Come on, Archie. Let's climb this tree." *If I climb high enough maybe all my problems will disappear.*

With both hands free, Eliza Jane took hold of each branch, climbing up one to the next until she went as high as she could go. The whole way up she thought about the things Ruby and Jacob had said to one another. *He's right. No one gets it.* She took a deep breath. *Except me.* She rolled her eyes but this time it wasn't because of a tic.

"Great Scott!" Archie whimpered. "Where are we going? To Mars? Do *not* let go." He swayed in his pouch every time she pushed upward.

"The strap is super strong, Archie. Don't worry." But, just in case, Eliza Jane held a hand under him every chance she got. She had climbed so high they could see the schoolyard in all directions.

"Look, I hate to tell you," Archie said, "but under my ferocious, brawny, remarkably fit Chihuahua physique, I'm a bit of a weenie. As in wimpy—not as in a wiener dog." He was talking faster than usual. "I can assure you I'm as full-bred as they come. A Chihuahua through and through. But here's the thing. When I'm too high off the ground, I turn into a great big scaredy-cat."

"You are *not* a scaredy-cat, Archie," Eliza Jane told him. "And not one bit wimpy either. You're the bravest dog I've ever known! And sweet as honey, too."

He went goo-goo eyed.

She nestled Archie into the crook of her arm. "Come here, sweet boy. You're safe in this pouch. I promise."

Then his eyes started riding waves.

"*Archie?*! Are you okay? You're looking woozy, boy."

His eyes slammed shut. "Please excuse me while I bury my head in your armpit." He twisted around and nudged his cold, wet nose under Eliza Jane's left pit and started boo-hooing like an actual weenie. And a great big scaredy-cat, too. Then he shrieked, "Get us down from here!"

"Archie Wa-wa," Eliza Jane cried. "Don't panic, boy. And don't faint!" She patted his head and wiped one sweaty palm against her pants, feeling a bit woozy herself. "We aren't *that* high up. Now—take a nice, slow, deep breath like I do when I have anxiety. In through your nose—out through your snout." She closed her eyes, demonstrating. But when she opened them, she spotted more trouble.

"Everyone's laughing at Jacob," Eliza Jane said. "And not in a nice way. What's going on?"

Archie stopped blubbering long enough to take a peek. His ears shot up like arrows, his hackles rising.

Eliza Jane wished she could make it stop. She wanted to say how bad it feels to be left out and picked on. But she didn't. Everyone watched and did nothing—including her. Fear swallowed her up and pinned her to the tree. She felt a giant wave of shame roll over the old maple.

"You can't expect yourself to be like anyone else— or them to be like you," Archie said. "That's the fun part—don't they know? Learning about each other's differences makes life an adventure! If only they understood that."

Eliza Jane sighed. *If only I could* say *that.*

Trills and warbles burst from the brilliant yellow belly of a western meadowlark, perched on a twig next to Archie and Eliza Jane. The dazzling bird screeched and carried on like she sensed something was wrong too. They all witnessed what happened next.

"Hey!" Ruby shouted. "Get your dopey arms out of my face!"

Jacob's arm sliced through the air like a sword. He looked like a school crossing guard directing traffic.

"My arms aren't dopey!" Jacob shouted back, his arms swinging around like a windmill.

"It looks like he's having a tic attack," Eliza Jane said. She picked at a piece of bark on the maple's trunk and ripped it off like a scab. Then she propped her chin in both hands and watched Jacob burrow his knees into his chest.

Eliza Jane knew Jacob had to be holding back an ocean of hurt. *This isn't right.* Even the meadowlark screeched and flew away as fast as her wings would carry her.

There was a bitter knot in the pit of Eliza Jane's stomach. *Now what do I do?*

Archie must have read her thoughts. "Stop them," he said.

"Me?" Eliza Jane said quietly. "Only a real-life Tinklelocks could do that."

4

## SAVED BY THE BIRDS

*J*ACOB had staggered back to the fire pole away from everyone when another hullabaloo started. It sounded like a stampede of cattle. Loud, rowdy voices bounced on the ground beneath the tree.

"Everyone has to keep this a secret," Eliza Jane heard someone say. "No one can tell anyone!" She peeked between maple leaves the size of pies and recognized the kids huddled below as fifth graders. *Thank goodness none of them are Ruby.*

"Yeah," a different voice said. "If anyone tells, we'll all be in big trouble."

"No one tattles, agreed? This might be dangerous."

*Dangerous?* Eliza Jane's heart sped up, her breathing rickety.

"Stay very still, or they might look up and see us," Archie whispered. "Become one with the tree."

"Here's the plan," someone continued. "We want to make Jacob mad enough so he'll leave and never come back."

"Exactly!" a different boy piped in. "Ruby's right. He's rude!" And then like some kind of big shot he called Jacob a name using the same hurtful word Ruby had. "She was right about that, too!" he hollered.

Eliza Jane cringed. She refused to use words like that to describe anyone. *Just because he's different, they act like Jacob's feelings don't even count. But everyone's feelings count!*

"I'm warning you," the same person continued, "Jacob can run superfast! We'll have to be faster. The question is how."

Other boys spoke up. "Let's knock him to the ground and steal his shoes and socks! That'll slow him down."

"Good idea."

A chill surged up and down Eliza Jane's spine. *Would they actually hurt Jacob?*

Archie hissed. "No-good scallywags. Nothing but a bunch of bullies."

"If he's barefoot, he won't get far," someone said. "But how do we get his shoes and socks off?"

"Easy! Twist his arm and push him down—works on my little brother every time. Do whatever you have to. Just hold him down."

*There's my answer.*

"We'll grab his shoes and socks, and you two steal his jacket laying by the swings."

Eliza Jane knew that any sound or motion might attract their attention upward, but she wanted to hide herself better. Carefully, quietly, she lay back, straightening her legs against the hefty branch, keeping a strong grip on Archie. Like a chameleon, she imagined she was perfectly camouflaged against the crusty old timber. The tree felt like armor, cradling them in a giant cuddle. She watched her ribcage heaving up and down under Archie's pouch, her heart knocking in her chest. She only hoped they couldn't hear it.

"Then what?" someone asked.

"Empty his pockets. Throw everything into the orchard as far as you can in different directions. He'll have to chase after his stuff. Remember, he'll be barefoot!"

When Eliza Jane heard them chuckling, it turned her stomach. *This has gone way too far.*

"Be careful," Archie whispered. "It's time to be calm. Don't let them know we're here."

*Become one with the tree,* Eliza Jane repeated to herself.

"Remember, get him as far out into the orchard as you can!"

"Then what do we do?"

"Take off and leave him there! He'll get the hint not to come around us again."

Eliza Jane's tics started.

*Please not my whistle. Not my throat sounds, either. Nooo. Please.*

Archie scooted his body over her neck. "Thank you, boy," she mouthed.

But the tics kept coming. She cleared her throat, whistling again and again, her eyes blinking, this time holding back tears.

*Stupid tics!*

She slowly lifted a hand over her mouth, hoping to muffle the sounds. She figured it was only a matter of time before they spotted her. She closed her eyes and begged. *Do not look up. Please, just walk away!*

But the voices lingered below. And the whistles continued. Her heart flip-flopped in her chest.

It wasn't until Eliza Jane lifted her eyelids that she caught sight of a miracle facing her—the yellow-bellied meadowlark was hovering right before her eyes. *She's back!*

The bubbly, vivid bird bounced and skittered about the branches, chirping every time Eliza Jane's whistle and throat sounds escaped. And then more birds came, all of them swirling in the air above her. Eliza Jane's tics blended in with their birdsong. And they never sounded more divine. *As beautiful as the songbirds.*

Eliza Jane wanted to tell all the birds, but especially the meadowlark, that they had saved her. She released silent gratitude, hoping they would feel it radiating from her heart.

*Thank you, thank you, thank you.*

"When Eliza Jane heard a commotion below, she spied through the leaves again. The bullies were finally leaving. They sprinted past Ruby, who was playing four-square on the blacktop. Eliza Jane watched her stop the ball as if she might leave the game to join them. But when the hooligans quickly disappeared, Ruby went back to playing.

"Come on, Archie," Eliza Jane said. "It's safe. They're gone, and Ruby's busy. We have to warn Jacob before it's too late."

"That's my girl!" he beamed. "Don't be a bystander. Be a defender!"

They scampered down the tree so fast Eliza Jane felt like they were flying. She closed her eyes and imagined swooping through the air, tilting to the right and then to the left, circling the playground like a drone! *I'm tired of being a bystander. I want to be a defender. It's what Tinklelocks would do!*

"Over there," Archie pointed. "Jacob's on the monkey bars." He bounded out of Eliza Jane's arms, prancing excitedly behind her all the way to where Jacob swung, one bar to the next.

"You don't know me," she said, looking up at Jacob. "But I'm Eliza Jane, and you have a problem. A *big* problem." She spoke between quick breaths. "Four bullies are after you and believe me, they mean trouble." Jacob dropped with a thud and Eliza Jane told him every last detail of the whole nasty, despicable plan.

"Wow," Jacob said. "I thought this school would be different. But it's not. It's worse than the last one."

"Sorry." Eliza Jane didn't know what else to say.

Jacob turned toward the swings. "My jacket's still there and so is my other stuff. Maybe they changed their minds."

"Maybe." But Eliza Jane didn't believe it when she said it.

"What'd they look like?" he asked.

Eliza Jane described them as best she could.

"Yup—they're all fifth graders," Jacob said. "They're in my class and so is that girl, Ruby. I just saw one of the boys grab a dog and run over there." He pitched his chin toward the cafeteria building.

"A dog?" Eliza Jane's forehead tightened. "They didn't have a dog."

"They do now."

"Huh…" Eliza Jane's eyes narrowed. "Wait a minute." She whipped around, flustered. "Where's my dog? He was just here!"

"I don't know," Jacob said. "I never noticed you had a dog." He scanned the area around them. "All I can tell you is they had one. A little black Chihuahua."

5

## TO THE RESCUE

"*T*HEY took my dog!" Eliza Jane struggled for breath. "Where are they?"

"That way!" Jacob pointed. "I'll help you find him. I promise."

Eliza Jane hurriedly skip-hopped in the direction Jacob had pointed, shouting, "Archie! Here, boy!" She released her words like a prayer—"Don't anyone hurt my dog. Give him back to me!"

*Come on, Tinklelocks.* It was wishful thinking because once again nothing happened when Eliza Jane twirled and whirled, spinning like a pinwheel. *What did I expect? She's not real.* She stormed ahead under a row of trees, her boots pounding the pine-needled pavement. She imagined magic prickling the soles of her feet granting her the power to sprint faster than she ever had before—as powerful as a turbojet. Eliza Jane would do anything to save Archie. And now she only hoped she could.

Jacob sped past her with ease.

*Oh, he is fast!*

"There they are!" Jacob pointed to a long hedge of blackberries. "I see them behind the bushes!" He turned toward Eliza Jane. "They must've taken your dog when they saw us together. I guess we spoiled their plan. I'm sorry. I think they took Archie because of me."

Eliza Jane shook her head. "They're the ones who took my dog. They're the only ones to blame!" And then she heard Archie in the distance, howling the most heartbreaking sound she had ever heard, like an abandoned pup in the night. "What are they doing to him?!" Her heart collapsed.

"Archie Wa-wa!" she cried. "I'm coming for you, boy!"
*I have to get to him.* Jacob followed Eliza Jane when she
charged through the blackberry bushes, razor-sharp
thorns stabbing her right and left, her heart beating faster
than she could count.

They scrambled out the other side of the prickly
hedge at the same time. "What happened to them?"
they both asked. There was no sign of anyone.

"I don't hear Archie anymore. I'm scared, Jacob.
What if they hurt him?" Eliza Jane's eyes blinked so
fast she couldn't see straight.

"They're mean enough to do it," he said.

"Archie knew those boys were troublemakers. He only
chased them because he wanted to help us." Eliza Jane's
tummy sank. She knew sometimes Archie believed he was
a five-hundred-pound grizzly bear instead of a five-pound
nugget on twiggy legs. Just thinking about it stirred up
her tics again. *What if I never get him back?*

Jacob took a few steps forward, shoulders shrugging,
his neck twisting. "There!" he pointed. "They just ran
through the gate."

"With Archie?!" Eliza Jane teetered on the tips of
her toes, trying to catch a better view.

"No." Jacob drooped. "I didn't see your dog with
any of them."

The bullies dashed into the orchard, scrambling
between the rows of trees, hazelnuts crunching under

33

their shoes. It didn't take long before the orchard gob-
bled them up and they vanished.

Eliza Jane swallowed back fear. "Archie's gotta be here
somewhere. They must have hidden him." She rushed
about, sifting through the bushes and weeds with a sharp
eye, her feet trampling the tawny thicket and fiddlehead
ferns. Jacob searched too. They hunted everywhere for
him. And still, Archie was nowhere in sight.

"What if they buried him?!" The idea made Eliza Jane's
insides squirm. She bent down, inspecting the ground.

"I don't think they had time to do that." Jacob leaned
down, his face full of doubt. "I hate to say it," he said,
wiping the sweat trickling off his brow. "But they must
have taken him after all."

His words punched Eliza Jane in the chest. She had
to remind herself how to breathe.

"I hate to say this too." Jacob fiddled with his cap,
pushing it up and down over his forehead. "But one
guy had a big pocket on the front of his red sweatshirt.
Maybe that's where Archie was."

Eliza Jane couldn't shake the unhappy feeling he was
right. "Then I'm going after them." Her voice cracked.
"Archie needs me as much as I need him." Tears flooded
her eyes as she bolted past Jacob, plowing through
the shrubs and out the gate where she tripped over
something.

"Jacob!" she yelled. "Is this your jacket?" She picked it up.

34

"How did it get out here?" Jacob rushed to Eliza Jane's side. "Dumb question. We know exactly how it got out here. And there's my gum and candy, too. And my key!" He scooped his things up and jammed them in his pants pocket. Then he smirked. "At least I still have my shoes and socks on."

"They haven't given up their plan, Jacob. Only now they want *both* of us to follow them into the orchard."

Jacob wrapped his fingers around Eliza Jane's upper arm. "I'm the fastest runner in my class. Come on," he said, his whopping blue eyes pleading. "Let's go save your dog—run!"

"Stop," Eliza Jane held up her hand. "We don't have to run—"

"We do!" Jacob's voice grew stronger. "And we need to hurry!"

"No, we don't. I have a horse, Jacob. He can outrun anyone. Even you."

Jacob's eyes widened. "That's *your* horse tied to the tree?"

Eliza Jane nodded. "We're about to ruin their plan again. And believe me, my horse will go as fast as I ask him to. We can ride—"

"*We?*" Jacob's face lost all its color. "I've never ridden a horse before."

"Well, now's your chance. If you want to, I mean. He's the best horse I've ever known and I've been riding since I was four years old. You don't have to do anything except hang on to me, but if you don't want to, I'll understand. Honest."

"No, they kidnapped your dog! I want to help." Jacob's smiling eyes showed he was still on her side.

Eliza Jane skip-hopped to the tree. "Meet Popcorn," she said, busily untying his rope. "He went blind from a medical condition. He lost both his eyes a couple years ago."

Jacob's own eyes bugged out. "He lost his eyes?!"

Eliza Jane nodded. "We couldn't save them. He was in too much pain, so—"

"Wait. You ride a horse with *no eyes*?"

6

## A HORSE LIKE NO OTHER

"*P*OPCORN doesn't need eyes anymore," Eliza Jane explained. "He sees with his heart."

"But how? How can anyone ride a horse with no eyes?" Jacob's neck twitched and so did his face. "That can't be safe—"

"He's the safest horse alive. Honest." Eliza Jane dug for more carrots out of Archie's pouch. "He's trained to do everything he's always done and more." As soon as she brought a carrot to Popcorn's muzzle, he chomped it down in a frenzy. Eliza Jane swiped a wet, slobbery hand against her jeans. "It's hard to explain, but Popcorn and I trust each other—we're connected by something deep inside each of us that no one else can see. My mama's right—we're soulmates."

"That's cool. It really is… but…" Jacob hesitated again, panic rising in his voice. "I'm still getting on a horse that can't see a thing?!"

"Well yeah, no eyes means there's nothing to see with, Jacob." Eliza Jane massaged one of Popcorn's empty eye sockets. "Look, I know it sounds crazy riding a horse with no eyes, but trust me, he can see. Mainly by listening. He can hear the corners of his stall, where the barn door is, the trees surrounding us, the wide-open field. He senses where he is. And if he's unsure, he trusts me to show him. And right now he knows you're here and senses everything about you."

"Then he knows I'm afraid."

"He does. And he understands. It's Popcorn's abilities, not his disability, that make him special. If you want to ride with me, put this on." She held out her helmet. "But really, I understand if you'd rather not."

With one quick flick of his wrist, Jacob took the helmet from her hand. "I'm going," he said, fastening the strap under his chin. "I don't break my promises."

Eliza Jane led Popcorn to the fence, stuck a boot into the chain-link, and boosted herself up, swinging over the top of him. "Take my arm and do the same thing, Jacob. I'll help pull you up." He slipped and struggled a few times but finally grabbed hold and settled in behind her. "Now wrap your arms around my waist. I'll show you what he can do. And no worries. If you start to slide sideways, Popcorn will stop and lean the other way to protect you. He feels *everything*. He'll keep us both safe. I may be his eyes, but he's my protector."

"But he's so big," Jacob said. "Are you sure we should—"

"Yeehaw!" Eliza Jane blasted. The big horse lurched forward and Jacob's arms tightened around her. Popcorn took on speed, and a moment later they had burst away from the school and into the quiet orchard. "I'm coming for you Archie!" Eliza Jane sucked in mouthfuls of air. "We're on our way!"

She had to admit, the thrill of the chase gave her a wild rush of pride. Not only had she made it her mission to save Archie, but she was also doing it with a new friend. The whole thing made her feel plucky— the word her mama used that meant courageous.

"Wow!" Jacob said. "It's like he really has eyes."

"Told you so!" Popcorn never failed to impress. "Find the bullies, boy. We need Archie back." She gave him a squeeze and off he went into a full gallop across the orchard floor—trampling hazelnuts, dandelions, twigs, stones, weeds, clumps of moss, and leaves. Popcorn ran the race with ease.

And it didn't take long to find the scallywags. "I see 'em!" Eliza Jane shouted. "Keep going, Popcorn! Straight ahead." His hoofs clomped noisily on the hard dirt, closing in on the group. When the circle of kids turned, their jaws dropped as they caught sight of Popcorn barreling toward them. They were speechless.

Eliza Jane pulled back the reins, bringing Popcorn right up alongside the fifth graders, her eyes inspecting the boy in the red sweatshirt. "Where is he?" she demanded. "I want my dog!" She watched for movement under his front pocket. "Tell me! Which one of you has him?"

At that point a heart-wrenching sound startled Eliza Jane. She pulled the reins to the right and wheeled around. First, she heard a high-pitched squeak. Then a faint cry. "I hear him, Jacob," Eliza Jane said. "That's Archie." It was, without a doubt, the sound of her precious pup bawling his eyes out. Her eyes prickled with tears too.

Someone slowly stepped out from behind a stocky hazelnut tree, its mossy branches snaking in the air toward them like three long, crooked fingers.

Eliza Jane blinked and rolled her eyes so many times she wasn't sure she was seeing things right.

"Ruby?!" It was Ruby all right. And she was holding Archie, his marble-black eyes peeking out from her folded arms.

Eliza Jane's eyes sparked fire. "How did *you* get here?!"

Jacob nudged Eliza Jane's arm. "Look," he muttered. Ruby's bike lay sprawled across the dirt between a row of trees. "She caught up to them when we were searching for Archie."

Eliza Jane's face turned the color of a radish. "How could you, Ruby?!"

"Relax—the dog's fine," she said, turning to the others. "Hey everyone, Eliza Jane actually speaks! This is the first time I've heard her say anything."

Eliza Jane straightened. "I should've known you were a part of this." Her set jaw was tight with fury.

"It's not my fault he was wandering around lost!" she spluttered. "The boys found him and I was only trying to help."

"He was not lost, Ruby. And you know it. Give me my dog."

"I said he's fine. Stop worrying."

Archie's eyes doubled in size, glued to Eliza Jane.

"I said, give me my dog," Eliza Jane repeated. "I'm warning you. My horse doesn't behave well around mean people. He won't be nice to any of you."

"What—you have an attack horse?" The whole gang practically fell over laughing.

*This will show them!* Eliza Jane whispered over her shoulder, "Hang on, Jacob," then reared Popcorn up, his hoofs swiping fearlessly in the air.

"Whoa—" They all stumbled backward.

Eliza Jane signaled Popcorn to slowly circle them.

Jacob taunted: "Ever been bitten by a horse with no eyes?! It's not pretty."

Eliza Jane's eyebrows shot up, but she kept her mouth shut.

The bullies exchanged glances. "He's right. Look!" someone said. "There's nothing in his eye sockets!"

"Gross!" they all chimed together.

"That is *so* creepy." Ruby shivered but cradled Archie affectionately in her arms.

*Wait. Is Ruby actually hugging my dog?*

Ruby stepped toward Eliza Jane, gazing adoringly into Archie's eyes.

*Ruby looks lovesick. She has stars in her eyes!* But as quickly as they appeared, they were gone.

"Okay, fine," Ruby said, handing him over. "Take your little rat. He's a pain anyway."

That was a big, fat fib. Eliza Jane knew he was the easiest dog who had ever lived.

Archie leapt into Eliza Jane's arms with such gusto, she thought he had sprouted wings! He was shaking like jelly.

"Let's go." Ruby turned on her heel, sulking when she picked up her bike.

The pack of bullies torpedoed away and didn't look back.

Archie tucked his tail between his legs and muttered in Eliza Jane's ear: "Ruby was actually very kind. Quite fond of me, in fact. I must say, I sensed she may have had a little 'doggy-crush' on yours truly."

"What?" Eliza Jane kept her voice low. *How dare she.*

"Okay. It wasn't 'little.'" Archie flashed a toothy grin at Eliza Jane so fast, she almost missed it. "The truth is, the girl fell for me. And she fell hard. But she wasn't *you*. I was terrified I'd never see you again!" Then he collapsed in Eliza Jane's arms and fainted.

"Archie! Come back! I'm right here boy," Eliza Jane said, fanning his face. She felt a rush of love, relieved to feel his heart thumping.

"He's limp as a rag," Jacob said, leaning over Eliza Jane's shoulder. "Poor thing."

Eliza Jane hugged Archie tighter, her voice shaking. "Do you think there's any danger of him dying?"

Jacob shrugged. "Dogs do sometimes croak suddenly."

Archie looked like an angel already, his head on Eliza Jane's lap, overpowering sweetness on his little black face. "Come back, Archie," she begged. "Don't leave me, boy. Please come back."

*If my essential oils can help my tics—maybe they could help Archie...* Eliza Jane dug around in her front pocket, uncapped the tiny gold bottle, and whisked it under Archie's snout. She took a whiff too, just in case. He woke up with a jolt, his tail wagging furiously. "It worked!" She covered his face with merry kisses. Archie was her everything.

They took their time on the ride back to the school playground. The air sweetened when Eliza Jane passed under a cherry tree in bloom, its umbrella of pink blossoms like perfume to her nose. She turned and met Jacob's eyes. "I'm lucky you're my friend. Thanks for helping."

A lopsided smile swept across his face.

"And," Eliza Jane added, "that was *so* smart to tell them that Popcorn bites!"

"*Does* he really bite?"

She hooted. "Only carrots! Popcorn is nothing but gentle and friendly to everyone. But they didn't need to know that."

"Nope," Jacob snickered, adjusting his ball cap. "Popcorn sure has a brave heart."

"So do you, Jacob."

His head twitched and then his shoulders shrugged. "Nah."

"Seriously?" Eliza Jane's mouth fell open. "You just rode bareback on a big blind horse chasing a pack of bullies!"

Jacob's face glowed. "True."

*Come to think of it, so did I.*

Eliza Jane led her magnificent horse with no eyes back to the playground. "Good boy, Popcorn," she said, leaning forward, her face buried in his thick, shiny mane, arms wrapped around his neck. "You saved Archie. You're a *real* superhero." She heard Ruby in the distance, playing a game of tag. *Good—she'll leave us alone.*

"I gotta go home after I get all my stuff," Jacob said. He dropped to the ground, patted Archie's head, and then stroked Popcorn's neck. "Thanks for the ride, boy. Sorry I doubted you." Jacob darted through the gate shouting, "See you Monday, Eliza Jane!"

"Okay! Thanks again for helping me." Eliza Jane hesitated. "Hey Jacob?" He turned to listen, stepping slowly backward. "I think I know what you were trying to say at the fire pole to Ruby and the others," she said carefully. "Sometimes people get confused and scared just because someone's different, and I noticed you have—"

She stopped talking when Jacob scurried away toward the swings, waving goodbye as if he hadn't heard a thing. But she knew he did. She believed he heard every word.

Eliza Jane had no idea why Ruby did what she did next.

7

## MOXIE MAGIC

"*L*ET'S ride, boys. Time to go home." When Eliza Jane asked Popcorn to leave, he cantered eagerly into the orchard. "*Good boy*," she said with love in her voice.

Barely fifteen seconds had passed on the dusty path when Archie said, "Not so fast, guys."

"What do you mean?"

"It's Ruby and the bullies. Remember, I have the perfect view back here. I think they're up to no good again. Something's happening."

"To Jacob?"

"Yes."

"*Again?!*" Eliza Jane felt her cheeks get hot.

"I'm afraid so. Guess they didn't count on getting busted by a clever dog such as myself who is watching their every move." And then with new urgency, Archie ordered: "Back to the playground! *Now!*"

They spun around and trotted swiftly to the schoolyard gate.

As soon as Eliza Jane's boots hit the ground, she knew what was happening. Ruby had Jacob's blue baseball cap in her hand, taunting him. But instead of rushing to Jacob's side, as any good friend would do, Eliza Jane darted straight to the old maple and hid. Her tics ran wild.

*Jacob's a friend now. A good friend! I should help.* She bent down and let Archie jump to the ground from his pouch.

"Are you sure you want to hide like this again?"

"Yes, Archie! I want to hide again, *okay?*" It was a lie and Archie knew it.

"Simmer down. It's just that Jacob—"

"I know! Jacob helped us! I know that, and I know I should do something, okay? But my tics are really bad and I can't!" Eliza Jane blew out a noisy gust of air. "I just can't...."

Jacob lurched toward Ruby's hand trying to snatch his cap back, but she flicked it away. Over and over, she dangled the cap like a prize, flicked it back again, and watched Jacob grasp at the air. Everyone giggled. Then someone stuck out their foot and tripped him. He stumbled, dropping hard to the ground. Jacob clutched his arm in pain, grimacing. "Ow!" he yelled. Then his neck twisted repeatedly. "Ow! Ow! Ow!" he cried out.

Eliza Jane had seen enough. With a wildness in her eyes, she twirled and whirled, spinning like a pinwheel, determined to transform. *Maybe it will work this time!* But it didn't.

Eliza Jane slumped down next to Archie. "It never works. Now what do I do? Popcorn can't help me—he'd never fit through the gate. I'm nothing but a chicken without him."

"Magic words might help," Archie suggested.

"That's an idea." *But what magic words?* Eliza Jane's face scrunched up as she tried to think. And then she blew out all the air in her lungs. "It's no use, Archie. Magic isn't real and neither is my inner secret superhero."

In that moment, a cloud of pixie dust floated through the air, covering Eliza Jane with a golden glow. How was it possible? Later, Jacob told her that her hair and clothes were coated in yellow tree pollen. Pollen or pixie dust—it didn't matter. The real magic happened when she looked up and did what she did next. Her eyes fluttered and she whistled out a soft tic as delicate as a tinkling chime.

"That's it!" Eliza Jane started twirling and whirling, spinning like a pinwheel again. Then she recited, "Tinkle, tinkle, hear my whistle!" Before she could say it twice, a tornado of green glitter engulfed her.

Eliza Jane couldn't believe what happened next. She felt a soft mask on her face, her fingertips sparkling green after she touched it. "This is amazing," she gulped. When her feet came into focus, she could hardly believe her eyes. Her brown tattered cowgirl boots had turned into gleaming black leather boots and her jeans turned into sparkly green pants that matched a twinkling green top. She glittered like a tree full of fairy lights.

Eliza Jane felt crazy cool. But all Archie said was, "*Whoa.*"

Next thing she knew they were flying. Archie and Eliza Jane shot into the air so fast her tummy did a somersault. She couldn't help but notice that her straight brown hair had changed into the color of sunlight. She swept long, flowing locks of golden ringlets from her face, hugged Archie tight, and kept running. Well—*flying*.

That was the moment a red-hot ball of courage burst open inside Eliza Jane's chest. *Kablooey!* It pinged up to her head and made her brain buzz. Then it flew all the way down to her toes. *Whooosh!* Brave feelings unspooled inside her. And just like that, Tinklelocks was ready to roll. This time she was real.

She held Archie tight and shot by everyone so fast, heads were spinning. People must have seen stars. The two of them were nothing but a blur of green glitter.

"I do say," Archie said. "Tinklelocks has moxie."

"I do? I mean—she does?"

"Oh, yes," he said. "True moxie."

"What does moxie mean?"

"Courage. Daring. Real guts."

Eliza Jane tried the word out, softly. "Moxie." Tinklelocks surely had guts. And courage. She was daring, too. Just what Eliza Jane wanted for herself. "Yes," she said louder. "MOXIE."

Archie barked. "It's time to do the impossible!"

*Wait—no one said it was impossible.* Once again worry crawled into Eliza Jane's brain. So did the same wimpy, great big scaredy-cat Archie had talked about. It crept in and tiptoed right up her spine.

But then Eliza Jane remembered Tinklelocks was in control. Anything was possible for a superhero.

Her black leather boots felt real when she skidded through the dirt and landed in front of the crowd of kids surrounding Jacob. Heart thumping in her chest, she commanded, "Stop in the name of Tinklelocks!" and slammed her boots down in front of them, blocking their escape.

She kept a big eye pinned on them. *Tinklelocks is brave. Maybe I am too.*

Archie leapt from her arms in a frenzy, prancing in circles.

Kids from all over the playground gathered and nosed in close, all of them staring wide-eyed at "Tinklelocks." But it was still plain ol' ordinary Eliza Jane standing right there in front of them with her inner superhero. Her knees were quivering.

"Tinklelocks?!" They all burst out laughing. "Your name is Eliza Jane," Ruby hooted.

"Of course it is," Eliza Jane said. "But this time you get Tinklelocks too." Heads tipped sideways, all of them bug-eyed and staring as if she were a tricky math problem standing in front of them. "You guys need to stop this. You hurt my friend! The best kind of friend there is. Jacob isn't rude," she said. "But you are, just because you don't understand why he's different. You treat him like his hurt feelings don't even count. But they do. Everyone's feelings count! And, *news flash*—not all people act the same way. Every single one of us is different!" Her speech came out wilder than she had planned. And it felt great. So she continued: "You can't expect yourself to be like anyone else—or them to be like you. That's the fun part—don't you know? Learning about each other's differences makes life an adventure!" Archie's hind end wiggled with pride when she said it. "Jacob tried to explain things to you, but no one gave him a chance. So now you're going to listen. If you don't, I'll squeeze Popcorn right through that gate and—well, trust me, it won't be pretty."

"He's a biter!" Jacob shrieked.

Eliza Jane couldn't help but notice that her throat was completely unclogged and all her words were flying out like rockets.

That's when Jacob stood like a tower of strength and faced everyone.

8

## TWO HEROES WITH TICS

LL play halted. Even the woodpecker jack-hammering on a nearby tree quieted. So did the flutter of wings and clicks and chatter of the birds overhead.

"I was born with Tourette syndrome," Jacob announced. "It's different for everyone, but I repeat sounds or words over and over and make sudden body movements—even if I don't mean to. They're called tics. That's why I might seem rude or look funny sometimes, but it's not on purpose!" Jacob said. "I can't help it."

"Of course you can't," Eliza Jane said. More kids crowded in to hear what he was saying. Even the boy in the red sweatshirt sat and listened. Jacob was as popular as the monkey bars now.

"Tics are like hiccups that won't stop," he said. "Trying to hold them in is tough."

"It's okay to let your tics out whenever you need to, Jacob," Eliza Jane said. "They can be painful."

"Yeah," Jacob said. "When I yell 'Ow!' it's because my muscles move in ways they shouldn't, and it hurts a lot. Tic attacks are the worst." He sighed. "To be honest, some days I don't want to come to school at all." He stared down at his shoes and swept aside a bristly pine cone. "Sometimes after a hard day, I go home and explode. Tics make me angry sometimes too."

"He's 100 percent telling the truth," Eliza Jane said. "Athletes, movie stars, teachers, scientists, dancers, musicians—all kinds of people, young and old, have Tourette's. It's just another way of being different."

Jacob nodded.

"Tell them what they can do to help you, Jacob." Eliza Jane shot him a thumbs up.

"Be a good friend," he said. "Treat me the same way you treat everyone else. That's all."

Ruby was the first one to drop her head. "Sorry, Jacob. I had no idea. That sounds really hard and super painful." She reached out and gave him a hug. "If you give me another chance, I promise you won't be sorry."

When Jacob beamed, Eliza Jane knew he forgave her.

Like everyone, there was more inside Ruby than anyone knew. She planted her feet next to Eliza Jane. "I thought you were *so* shy. I was wrong about you, too."

"You were," Eliza Jane said. "But I am quieter than most—you were right about that. I'm just more of a thinker than a talker, that's all."

"Maybe you can change."

"But I don't want to change. I like being an introvert! I wouldn't change that for anything. It makes me happy being a deep thinker. You should try it." Eliza Jane liked the new habit of speaking her mind freely.

"The truth is," Ruby said, her eyes misty, "I didn't want to give Archie back to you because he was so sweet. That's the only reason I tried to keep him—honest. I took real good care of him."

"I know you did. He—I mean—thanks for telling me." Eliza Jane almost said Archie had told her already. "I'm glad you saw what a good boy he is."

"Do you want to walk across that big, old log together sometime?" Ruby asked. "Maybe you could teach me how to be a deep thinker too."

Eliza Jane noticed a twinkle in Ruby's smile when she told her, "Sure!"

Archie settled in Eliza Jane's lap. She kissed his velvety ears, and when she stroked his silky-smooth coat, he rolled over in bliss.

Ruby asked why Eliza Jane kept blinking up at the sky.

"I'm not," she said, clearing her throat a few times. "Big feelings usually make my tics worse." Eliza Jane grunted and made a soft little whistle, even though she didn't mean to.

A sea of startled faces turned her way, their eyes as big as baseballs.

"*You* have tics?" Jacob asked.

Eliza Jane nodded. "I have Tourette syndrome too."

"Wow!" Jacob grinned. "No wonder you know so much about it."

"There's plenty of days I wish I didn't," she told them. "But it's a part of me. Not all of me, but a part."

Eliza Jane's tics always worsened when she felt like she was in the spotlight. She pushed a hand over her mouth and her cheeks got hot, but at least she no longer wanted to run and hide. *So this is what it's like to be me. The honest-to-goodness, real-life, authentic Eliza Jane. I've shown her to everyone, thanks to Tinklelocks. I'm never going to stop being my true self again.*

"The truth is," Eliza Jane continued, "I wouldn't be who I am without Tourette's." As soon as she said that, she knew it was true.

"Why?" Ruby asked.

"Because having Tourette's is one way I'm different. And we all need differences to do unique and special things."

"Yeah, like being as brave as a superhero!" Jacob said. "We're two heroes with tics, Eliza Jane."

"We are," she smiled.

Archie whispered, "Being kind is brave too." He practically danced a jig when he bounded out of Eliza Jane's lap and scampered about, letting the gaggle of kids love on him.

THE LEAVES OF THE OLD MAPLE WERE SWAYING when Eliza Jane skip-hopped over the puddles of sunshine dotting the blacktop. Before she and Archie left the school grounds, she caught a reflection of herself in a classroom window. She pressed her nose to the glass to be sure it was her.

"It's me," she told Archie. And there she was—big brown eyes, rosy cheeks, and hair like hay.

*I sure don't look like Tinklelocks now.*

Gone were the silky, twisting golden curls of her imagination. She ran her fingers up through her bangs, making her hair stick up in spikes. It didn't help a thing.

But the funny thing was, a part of Eliza Jane still felt like Tinklelocks. She wasn't convinced her inner superhero had completely disappeared. Maybe, she decided, pretending to be strong, brave, and bold had actually made her that way.

Underneath her muddy jeans, scraped-up hands, dirt-stained T-shirt, and arms prickled like bloody pincushions from blackberry thorns, Eliza Jane was the same ten-year-old girl. And yet not the same.

Eliza Jane adjusted Archie's pouch on her back. He snuggled in when she mounted Popcorn with one strong kick off the tree. Archie gave everyone a wink, and in a flash they were gone. But Tinklelocks would be back. Because in the golden light of that sparkling spring day, Eliza Jane learned that she was a part of her—not all of her, but a part. It warmed her heart knowing Tinklelocks was always there inside her, ready to help.

The meadowlark watched as Eliza Jane rode home with a new sense of freedom, her heart like a tree bursting into bloom. The sun flooded her face with warmth when a whistle, soft as a tinkling chime, escaped from her lips.

*Hear my whistle, everyone! Hear ME.*

# A Note from the Authors
## *With gratitude*

Tourette syndrome is one of the most misunderstood medical conditions. Yet it's more common than most people realize. In fact, according to the Tourette Association of America, 50 percent of all children with Tourette syndrome go undiagnosed.

Being neurologically different does not diminish a person's worth—not their talent, passion, intelligence, or heart. Nevertheless, many children experience embarrassment, shame, and bullying due to their tics. Physically and emotionally, attempting to suppress or mask this condition is extremely painful.

Our hope is that *Eliza Jane Finds Her Hero* will raise awareness, create more understanding and acceptance, and help increase support for all who live with Tourette's and for all those who go undiagnosed.

We want to thank those who have followed our writing journey. Without your support, this book would not be here.

Thank you to family and friends who cheered us on, offered feedback, and brainstormed ideas with us. We love you.

To author and book editor Ellen Notbohm for her gift of time and for finding us the perfect title! We are so grateful to you.

To our illustrators, Patti Culwell and Jazlin Sobel, whose superb talent shines on the cover and throughout this story. We applaud you.

To our publishers, Luminare Press, for their guidance, and professionalism. You gave us a book we love.

And finally to you, the reader. We're honored you have this story in your hands.

With gratitude,
*Eliza and Debra*

# More Information for Kids and Families

## The Tourette Association of America (TAA)
www.tourette.org

This national organization works to raise awareness, advance research, and provide ongoing support to parents and families impacted by Tourette syndrome and tic disorders. Its mission includes fostering social acceptance; investing in research;educating professionals; providing support, hope, and help;and empowering the community.

## Tourette / Kids Quest / CDC
www.cdc.gove/ncbddd/kids/tourette.html

The CDC website on Tourette syndrome tells you the facts, signs, causes, treatment, and what to do if you're concerned about someone with tics.

## Tourette's Action
www.tourettes-action.org.uk

The UK's leading support and research charity working to improve the lives of people living with Tourette syndrome. Services include online live chat and email support, a befriender network, information, webinars, events, and resources. It also organizes conferences and hosts adventure holidays for teenagers.

## NJCTS – Nation's First Center of Excellence for Tourette syndrome
www.njcts.org

The mission of NJCTS is to ensure children and adults with Tourette syndrome are empowered and accepted through education, advocacy, and research.

## Joshua Center for Neurological Disorders
www.joshuacenter.com

The Joshua Center is a nonprofit organization that provides services and support for the social, emotional, and educational needs of neurologically impaired children and their families, including children with Tourette syndrome, high-functioning autism, obsessive-compulsive disorder, and ADHD.

## Joshua Center Camp
www.campsforkids.org

*ACA accredited camp / overnight camp / specialty camp*

The Annual Joshua Center Residential Camp is a residential camp experience held at the Rotary Youth Camp in Lee's Summit, Missouri, for children with Tourette's, high-functioning autism, ADHD, and OCD.

# Child Neurology Foundation

www.childneurologyfoundation.org

Nonprofit advocacy organization located in Minneapolis, Minnesota, committed to serving as a collaborative center of education and support for children and families living with neurologic conditions.

# National Institute of Neurological Disorders and Stroke

www.ninds.nih.gov

Comprehensive information about Tourette syndrome including diagnosis, treatment, latest updates, and clinical research trials.

# About the Authors

**ELIZA KELLEY** is the owner of the true-life Archie—the most enchanting dog ever—who stars in this story. Eliza was diagnosed with Tourette syndrome when she was eight years old. She hopes this story will help others

better understand tic conditions. Eliza loves to ride horses (including one with no eyes!), climb trees, create art, play tennis, swim, and perform gymnastics. Archie is her greatest love, but she has a big heart for all puppies, cats and dogs. One day she hopes to live on a farm and become a horse trainer. This is her first published book.

**DEBRA WHITING ALEXANDER** holds a PhD in psychology and is the author of many non-fiction and fiction books, including award-winning novels *Zetty* and *A River for Gemma*. Her work has won the Will Rogers Medallion Award, Sarton Women's Book Award, 2018 WILLA Literary Award in Contemporary Fiction, Eric Hoffer Award for Legacy Fiction, and many more. She lives near the hazelnut orchards in Oregon where she loves taking walks with the coauthor of this book—her beloved, wildly creative granddaughter.

To contact Debra or Eliza please visit:
**www.debrawhitingalexander.com**

# About the Illustrators

**PATRICIA CULWELL** and **JAZLIN SOBEL** are a Pacific Northwest mother/daughter artist team in Oregon.

To contact them or learn more about their work please visit:
**www.theellart.com**

Made in the USA
Middletown, DE
09 November 2023

42240187R00046